The Downing Street Cats

A feline tail of the most "purrfect" stories of three extraordinary cats who happen to live at one of the world's most famous addresses.

About the author

Neil Sean is seen daily around the world on television as an entertainment / royal / political reporter and thanks to numerous days and hours positioned outside Number Ten Downing Street has become very well acquainted with the staff, police and most importantly the Downing Street Cats

Written / Produced / Arranged by Neil Sean

A Maycon Production

Assisted by Michael Dias

The following work is imagined from the perspective of the Downing Street Cats and any names / titles or similar incident are purely incidental.

"The Downing Street cats" tells the story of a gang of cats and their charismatic leader, Palmerston. With their ability and mischief, Palmerston will always try to rise above the cat fighting and paw-dropping clangers the other two do.

He always eats for free, thanks to the ever ready presence of the world's media on his doorstep. He also enjoys playing jokes on the staff including the Prime Minster, but he is always being watched by Chief of Police at Downing Street. PC Eric might be strict with them at times, but in fact is a friend to them all.

A personal message from Palmerston-

Dear reader. Before we go any further I want to share with you a top secret. Something that you must keep between you and I.

What you're about to read are elements of my secret dairies and blogs. You see, I am not just any ordinary rescue cat. I didn't wile away my time sleeping and eating while at Battersea. I took full advantage of their online training and language courses. So while humans think I am just your normal domestic cat, I can in fact fully understand how to operate a laptop, Twitter and Facebook and because of my extra skills, I have taken it upon myself to show true leadership and take on the running of this great country of ours. As you will see from my various jottings, the PM has been more than happy with some of my decisions so far. But as I say, keep this a secret as I am really a one-off special cat. Thank you for keeping my secret.

Meet Palmerston

As I surveyed the waiting press and media I let out a huge yawn and stretched out across the Downing Street pavement.

"Oh no!" I thought to myself.

"David promised a trip to the cattery but seems to have forgotten about me in his rush to leave. My personal look is ever so important you know."

I looked around and saw my soon-to-be ex-boss on the steps of Number Ten looking dashing and healthy in his smart blue suit along with his model-looking wife and children. I took the opportunity to people-watch once again.

I noticed a rather worn-out looking presenter from Sky News who it appeared was not an animal lover; each time he had made his way over in the past she had shooed me away. Naturally, I delighted in trying to trip her up while circling between her legs. Along with her worn out shoes she also had a huge ladder in her stockings. I swiped at her other leg in order to make

another ladder to match the first one, but she began to get angry.
"Go away you smelly thing, just go away!" she hissed in her strong Wigan accent.

Rushing back to my favourite spot between the doors of Number Ten and Number Eleven, I once again took a long view at the crowd.
"Usual suspects" I purred to myself.

But then I spotted that rather nice grey-haired man from the BBC.

"Ah!" I thought, and made a beeline for him. I liked him because at Christmas when visiting the PM for a chat he always brought gifts for the Downing Street staff, and even for the pets. There was always a special tin wrapped up in that crinkly paper that I always liked to play with and shred with my claws.

Making my way over, I was pleased to see Mr Huw (as I liked to call him) was smiling and reaching out with his hand to welcome me.
"I wonder what treats he will have for me today?" I thought. Last time it was some beef jerky and some rather nice clumps of meat, even though they were a tad overcooked. I took a sniff towards Mr Huw's bag, and caught the unmistakeable aroma of tuna sandwiches.

As Mr Huw, who was wearing his new BBC coat and scarf (despite it been high summer) continued to stroke my fur, I took another opportunity to hiss at the Sky News reporter who had chided me away.

As I was being stroked by Mr Huw, I thought about just how much my life had changed since I was picked up from that cat home. Battersea was nice and warm, but nothing on this place.

The main difference here is there are a lot more visitors; some you welcome, some you don't. For instance, at the cat home people just wanted to stroke you, meet you, feed you. It took some time to get used to having to pose for the camera crews and photographers, plus of course making sure I look my absolute best, collar straightened, claws clean, and whiskers standing proud.

At the cat home, I could have an off day, I could relax, even sleep all day if I wanted.

Saying that, I am enjoying my new surroundings and in particular, my new sleeping arrangements. My boss things I sleep in my new basket, but once he's gone to bed, I find his 'in-tray' far more comfortable!

The cameras began clicking heavily which took Mr Huw's attention back to the matter in hand; his shots and if anyone would want a selfie with him.

I adjusted my whiskers with my rather grubby paw and looked back on the crowd all snapping and shouting for the departing boss ... would he miss me?

Slowly walking back into the office I shared with some other ministers the newspaper headline on the desk caught my eye. 'Claws out, it's all kicking off in Downing Street. After a month of drastic change and bubbling tensions among Westminster's big beasts, things have started to turn violent.'

"Ah. It appears my recent scrap with Larry has hit the papers. Is nothing private anymore?" I pondered while looking decidedly annoyed at the picture of my feline counterpart Larry who it appeared had got a bigger picture in the spread.

Who is Larry?

Larry is the 10 Downing Street cat and is Chief Mouser to the Cabinet Office. Larry is a brown and white tabby, and has quickly developed a reputation for being late to attend meetings and aggression towards news reporters.

I find this rather annoying because I'm younger and yet far more dignified when it comes to public situations. The ex-Chancellor had stated to some visiting dignitaries that I was the "ultimate cat and the best mouse catcher they had ever had," something that had clearly upset Larry, who had been here for a few years.

For me, this historical and eventful day started as all my days do; I had a good stretch out and took time to look around the new posh office. I knew it was going to be a sad day as my boss, Mr Phil, was soon to depart. I was about to give my right paw a customary lick but was alarmed to see my suspected new boss Mr Boris on the front page of the tabloid newspaper. "He looks alright I suppose," I thought, "but I'm concerned about him bringing that other cat perched on top of his head into our surroundings".

There are only so many new chaps a chief mouser in my position could take under my wing. I remember a shocking incident earlier in the spring when partaking in my afternoon dish of chilled milk I overheard people speaking in whispering voices and repeating the word 'Trump'. This Trump person must be someone rather important as it was followed with the words 'no, no, no!'
I made a mental note to log onto the boss' laptop once he'd left for the day, to look up this man himself. Big mistake.

Just as I decided to stretch out, move forward and debate breakfast, I spotted Gladstone the cat. It seemed he'd not taken notice of my stern words about him sticking to his own patch. I stared long and hard out of the window and thought about how I would deal with this problem once I'd eaten breakfast. I was about to jump down from the desk when I noticed a lone reporter across the street; the new girl from Good Morning Britain. That was the problem with this new home; I was forever being woken up by people talking to themselves outside the front door. And literally having seen the ratings for Good Morning Britain, I knew that this really was the case.

I briefly met the original reporter for the show called Miss Sue. She was a lovely lady who was forever bringing some of those rather expensive pouches of cat food. Not the cheap stuff, no, that always comes from Channel 4. But this stuff has a rather nice picture of a lady cat on the packet, a little airbrushed perhaps, but nonetheless perfect.

Breakfast consisted of some of the nice choice cuts from last night's farewell dinner at Downing Street, (although the turkey was a little bit dry) and my soon to be ex-boss has been on a strict diet recently and that low fat skimmed milk didn't always hit the mark thirst-wise.

It was at this point that I decided to trot across for my now daily constitution and have a look around the cabinet war rooms. Here I'd already made friends with a couple of feline associates who held a similar position to me but of course they lived in a museum while I live at the cut and thrust of the action.

Just as I was about to step out, PC Eric scooped me up and gave me an obligatory pat on the head. Something I am not at all keen on. I liked PC Eric as while he was slightly bossy, I did feel sorry for him having to stand outside in all weathers.

Hang on though, I thought. What's happening here? PC Eric was removing my favourite collar and replacing it with a new one. While doing so he said: "you're going to have to look extra smart today young sir, as the worlds' media are all going to be out in force. And we don't this scruffy old collar on you do we?" And with one swift action, the collar was removed and a brand new one placed around my neck.

I wasn't keen as it seemed a little tight. However, I did cheer up a bit when I heard the word 'chip'. "Mmmm, lunch" I thought, despite just having had breakfast. I decided to smile in Eric's direction, but that was soon removed when I realised the chip in fact was not my favourite kind but a microchip that the boss had said all three of the Downing Street cats must have. Thinking 'not for me", I jumped out of the policeman's hands and picked up speed across to the cabinet war rooms.

As the events of this busy day unfolded, I thought it would be easier for all concerned if I was to run through my day hour by hour, maybe even minutes. The events certainly caught me by surprise, to the point where I did wonder who was going to be serving my dinner that night. Here is my diary of that rather unusual day...

09.30am

Still reeling from the shocking news that it will be the last day when my current boss, Mr David. I'm trying not to show that I'm upset and purr around him each time he comes near. I can see though, he is sad, and it's more obvious by the fact that he's walked past my empty bowl four times now.

As I sat outside number 10 surveying the building media, I could hear sky news and Five News discussing why Mr David was humming directly after he'd resigned. I cocked my right ear in their direction. They seem to be making far more of it than it actually was. After all, who better than me to know just how stressful this job is?! Of course he's relieved.

09.44am
It's just flashed up on the TV screen that we will have a new Prime Minister by the end of today. I wonder if Larry and Gladstone are across the news as much as me? After all, like my boss says, we're in this together.

10.15am
The phone's been ringing non-stop. A cat can hardly get his head down for ten minutes for a nap. There's nowhere really to sit as there are boxes with removal stuff in. It seems everybody's excited about the goings on, the media outside are getting more and more, and each time I head out towards the door I'm scooped back up and told to stay inside.

10.45am
George from next door has popped in now. He looks worried too. Although unlike Mr David, he hasn't yet ordered a removal van. He was asking if he thought he may be kept on., people were all agreeing saying of course but Being a highly intelligent feline I know better.

11.15am

It's an odd job this you know. People assume you're happy with what's going on around you. But with all this coming and going I have to say it's making my tummy nervous and as I point out to PC Eric, I desperately do need to pay a call of nature.

11.25am

It always pays to hang around by the bins you never know what you'll find. This is how I discovered myself Larry and Gladstone have all been offered a deal to front a new multi-national campaign, on TV no less. Naturally, I'm annoyed. What other deals have I not been told about? Maybe we're not all in this together!

11.55am

Finally, there's some peace and quiet. All the staff are gathered in the TV room to watch Mr David's final ever Prime Minister's Questions. I have to say he does look dashing in his brand new Pal Smith designer blue suit. It's a shame though, he didn't have time to touch his locks up as I for one know no-one in politics likes the sight of any grey hair.

12.50pm

Judging by the laughter from the room, the boss appears to be doing well. Even grizzly Mr Jeremy has aid a couple of compliments. You can't help but notice though, the sadness in his eyes. While the others are all clinking glasses of champagne I literally sit by my bowl, waiting. It seems today everybody is forgetting about me and my thirst!

1.30pm

I have to say, Larry's not going to be too happy when I tip him off about the latest news. while taking a leisurely stroll across the boss's desk, my right paw accidentally activated the screen and what should pop up? Only his secret honours list. No mention of Larry though!

2.00pm

Boss will be back soon so take this opportunity to stroll over to tip Larry off about this latest news. After all, we don't want him breaking down with all the media outside, do we?

2.10pm

Larry's not taken the news well and decided to take it out on me,. All in front of the eyes of the press and world's media. Some people stated that I was goading him but I was merely trying to be a good pal. Off to lick my wounds.

3.00pm

It's just come to my attention that the boss won't be coming back. How annoyed am I? Steaming! I was expecting a leaving present. It seems that it's not just Larry who is annoyed with how the day is unfolding.

3.30pm

Gathering my thoughts now and it's funny to see all the boss' old stuff piled up in the corner. I haven't seen that picture of him laughing with Rebekah Brooks for ages. Well in fact, not since the night he ripped it off the wall in anger. I jump on top of the box for a closer look. There are more pictures including one with Andy Coulson. He came to a sticky end too. Ended up in prison I think. It has been an eventful period here.

3.50pm
Apparently we're going to have a new boss soon. She is on her way. I'm not happy about this; there are whispers that she doesn't like cats! Can anybody confirm this?!

4.00pm
I call a meeting with Larry and Gladstone at the back of Number 10 in the Rose Garden. For once we're not fighting and they all agree that I should take charge and find out more. Easier said than done.

4.15pm
In order to create a diversion, we all decide to walk across to the media area. There's an overweight foreign reporter who almost steps on Larry while clad head to foot in Primark. I have to say I'm pleased to see there is come class to the proceedings though. The ever delightful Fiona Bruce has rocked up. She knows a thing or two about antiques!

4.30pm
The new boss apparently is delayed. So in order to fill for time, as they say in the business, the press look towards more to point their cameras at. They're all being nice

now because they want me to do tricks on the pavement. I don't oblige s I don't want the new boss thinking I can be easily pushed around.

4.40pm
Don't you hate a show-off? Now back in the house, even though we'd all agreed Larry is out front, on his back, paws in the air, rolling around and no doubt grabbing tomorrow's headlines. This is not a good day.

5.00pm
I am sitting on the steps of Number 10. PC Eric is beside me and a bit nervous. He says to me "Very soon, you will have a new boss." I looked up at him and gave him my most angelic look. I thought to myself "and so will you, matey".

5.15pm
A car sweeps up and out steps my new boss. I have to say, I am impressed. She's well-dressed and her husband has a very nice suit on. Looks very expensive. Something I could get my claws into.

5.30pm

I've got a magnificent position here on the steps as my new mistress makes her way to the lectern to deliver her maiden speech. I cast an eye across all the media. She has them spellbound. Me though, I'm wondering how I will get to keep on running the country with such outlandish claims. And more importantly, is anyone going to remember it's time to feed me? It's tough being Palmerston the cat, running the country, controlling your boss. I'm just letting my new secret friends, like you, into a glimpse of the secret world of the Downing Street Cats.

Manufactured by Amazon.ca
Bolton, ON

25268970R00017